Where is my glove?

Story by Kathleen Stevens

Illustrations by Mark Weber

Dr. Judith Nadell, Series Editor

Outside, it was a cold day.

Derek put on his coat and scarf.

He put on his hat and one glove.

"Where is my other glove?" said Derek.

"Is it lost?"

"Look in your pockets," said Grandpa.

The glove was not there.

"Look by the coat rack," said Grandpa.

The glove was not there.

"Look in your backpack," said Grandma.

The glove was not there.

"Look in back of the couch," said Grandma.

The glove was not there.

"Where is my other glove?" said Derek.

"I think I lost it."

"Oh no!" said Derek.

"**Jack** has my other glove!"